IT'S MY LIFE

NEHA AGARWAL

Made with ♥ on the Notion Press Platform
www.notionpress.com

The book is dedicated to my parents and all my teachers
specifically my English teacher Mr. Melvin deDoncker
and Ms.P. Bano. Special thanks to all my family members
and to the ones who may not be present with me but
will always be in my heart and prayers.

Preface

School life is like a bud. When you enter the real world, the bud must grow, blossom, and spread its fragrance. Just as all flowers are unique, so is each blossoming into a flower with a distinct purpose and path. Some flowers have thorns, while others do not. Similarly, every person has a unique journey. Some achieve easily while others face more struggles. Life's journeys differ for everyone. Some goals are achieved, and some are not, but this shouldn't stop us from dreaming and aiming for new goals. We all need to break out of our shells and breathe freely.

> *It is very simple to be happy, but it is very difficult to be simple.*
>
> *-Rabindranath Tagore*

It was seventeen years ago, that Trisha and Sunny met. Trisha harshly said, "This is our last meeting, we will not talk or meet after this." Sunny insisted, "We can be friends at least?" Trisha knew that they could never be friends, they were soulmates and would always be. They parted ways. They did not know what fate had in store for them. Trisha always thought that if something adverse happened, she could cope with it. But she knew Sunny would not be able to overcome it.

It has happened in the past that Sunny had told Trisha, "if we can't live together at least we can die together." In another incident, during one of their meetings, Sunny in a state of frustration told Trisha, "It is better if I take my life." Trisha knew Sunny had a lot of responsibilities towards his family as well. She would never want Sunny to even think about "taking his life ever and anyone for that matter. At their last meeting, Sunny told Trisha,"

"We are too young to commit to each other now." We should both concentrate on our "studies and build a career. Trisha in a gullible way responded," We can get married and study together. Sunny answered," I am not settled now neither are you, how will I take your responsibilities? "Give me at least five years to prove myself and then get settled. Sunny pronounced that his priority is not her now. Trisha got offended and asked if her parents someday asked him for her, would he accept or say no and if her parents found another match for her, then what would she say? Trisha misunderstood Sunny when he said that his priority was not her now. But Trisha just wanted to know, if he was committed to her.

Trisha understood one thing that in the coming years, there is no certainty of what will happen. So, she thought it was better not to go ahead as of now. She knew that she was doing the worst thing ever. But perhaps she had no choice. By doing this she would destroy his personal life however his professional life would be intact. Trisha had always assumed that just because she was the eldest girl child in the joint family, she would be married off early. Though no one ever told her so. This was their last meeting. They turned and never looked back. Words once spoken, can't be taken back. They may be forgiven but not forgotten.

1
Childhood Days

This is the story of Trisha, a girl born and brought up in Central Kolkata (Calcutta) (present-day Kolkata). She was born in a joint family, and she was the first girl child in the family. She had two elder brothers, Vikrant and Aman. Trisha's mother used to tell her that her father always wanted a girl child after the two sons. He went to Taraknath Temple in Tarkeshwar, a Hindu temple dedicated to Lord Shiva situated in Hooghly district, West Bengal carrying two ghade (pots or pitchers) without slippers so that he is blessed with a girl child.

Everyone loved Trisha both brothers, Vikrant and Aman, no doubt adored her a lot. Vikrant, the eldest one was very protective and supportive. On the other hand, Aman, the elder one, was also protective but unlike Vikrant, he did not support Trisha for all her obdurate demands. Trisha very well knew that her parents and her two brothers were the four pillars of her life. She never had to come across any difficulty or answer for any wrong or mischief done by her. She would always find an easy escape because if Aman had to say something to Trisha, then either Vikrant or her parents would speak for her, if Vikrant had to say something then Aman or her parents would speak for her. If her parents, try to tell her something then her brothers would stand for her. So, in a way, she was a child and never wanted to grow up. She knew one thing very well that growing up is no fun at all. Unlike any other child who always want to grow older, she prayed to God that she always wanted to be a kid. She understands the fact that "With power comes responsibility." According to Trisha, she neither wanted power nor responsibility.

1. *Admission in School:*

Trisha's parents wanted to provide the best education to their children. Both brothers were already admitted to the best of schools. It was now Trisha's turn to go to school. In her childhood, she was a shy and quiet child. It was hard for her parents to get her admitted to a school as she would not utter a word when asked questions. Her parents took her to almost all the renowned schools in Kolkata (Calcutta) (present-day Kolkata), but in vain. Everyone in the family has almost hope of seeing Trisha in one of the best schools. There was a school near her home. A few of the family members recommended to get Trisha be admitted there. There was one person who not even once thought that Trisha would study in the best school and that person was none other than her mother, Pushpa.

One day, Trisha's mother went to drop her son, Aman to the school bus. The conductor told her, "Mam, you had asked for the admission forms of

the school. Today is the last day of submission." Without any hesitation, she boarded the school bus and reached the school. She filled out the form and started eagerly waiting for the response.

To the utmost surprise, the call for the interview came. Trisha with her parents reached the school. When Trisha was asked questions, this was the first time that she opened her mouth and answered the questions correctly. Both her parents were overwhelmed because Aman was studying in the same school, and it was one of the best schools.

1(i) Incident in School:

It is truly said, that when you find a solution to a problem, other pops up. Now, when Trisha finally got admission to a school, everyone started questioning how she would cope as the ratio of boys to girls was 4:1. But then, Aman was there and if Trisha were not able to cope, her parents would shift her to another school in the secondary level.

Trisha was no more a shy or introverted person. By the time she reached the third standard, she was as loquacious as a parrot. She would not stop at all and keep blabbering continuously. She would voice for each and everything. There was an incident in the third standard where the teacher told all the children to keep their mouths shut and study. The teacher warned the children to follow her instructions diligently. Trisha immediately turned around to pass something to her friend and the teacher noticed and raised her voice. Trisha started crying inconsolably. Trisha has been brought up in an environment where she has not heard high pitch or never witnessed anyone scolding her.

She kept weeping for a very long time. It became almost impossible for the teacher to console her and tell her to stop crying. At the parent's teachers meeting, the teacher narrated Trishna's incident and vowed that she would never scold Trisha leave about hitting her.

1(ii)All - rounder:

Trisha was growing up. She usually made friends with boys rather than girls. She would always connect better with boys than girls. It was not that she did not have any friends who were girls but if four friends are boys then there was one friend who was a girl. She found boys to be more loyal, helpful, and not jealous. She enjoyed their company and was always seen with them.

Growing up, she started reading in front of the class, playing sports, and actively taking part in co-curriculum activities in school.

In her seventh standard, a play was conducted and luckily, she was offered the role of a main character. She portrayed her part marvellously and everyone applauded her for her performance. A new and reformed Trisha was born. She emerged to be a fearless, outspoken and stubborn girl.

Trisha started taking an interest in a whole lot of things happening around her. She would try hands-on as many activities as she could. This attitude of trying and trying helped to gain a lot of confidence.

She started playing throwball, and basketball and took part in the high jump. She even played in the school choir. She with other girls took part in the Independence Day programme dance with five girls. She with other girls danced to a patriotic song Trisha's expression was so natural that the girl choreographed the song that the girl placed Trisha at the centre of the stage. Many girls seemed jealous, but Trisha paid no heed to them.

1(iii) *Adored by All:*

In the seventh standard, a new history teacher was appointed in the school. After a few lectures, she took a surprise test. Everyone was baffled as to what they would write in the exam. When marks came and results came out, most of the students scored in single digits. Some scored even two or three. Can you imagine someone who did not score at all? When Trisha's exam paper everyone was bewildered because she scored 17 out of 25. All her friends were taken back. Everyone started asking as to how got so good marks.

She was always in the good books of all teachers. Mathematics was the only subject in which scored terribly. She got marks by which she could merely pass even after studying day and night. She did not know she why say is hated maths and loved other subjects.

"*Knowledge without action is wasteful and action without knowledge is foolish - AI Ghazali*"

Trisha's father came to school to collect Aman and Trisha's report cards. After collecting both their report cards, Trisha met her English teacher, Mr. deDoncker Trisha's father asked how she was doing in her studies.

She is a good student and doing well. To this, their father commented, "She is not good at all in Maths, but both of my sons are brilliant In Maths." To which, Sir immediately replied,

"Trisha is better in English than her brother Aman. So please do not compare between two children or any two people."

Every individual is unique so don't compare. In an examination all questions are similar. But the answers answered are different.

"*Do what your purpose is. If you are a marigold, you will be a marigold, if you are a rose you will be a rose. So don't change for anyone.*

-Gaur Gopal Das"

1(iv) Faith in God:

Trisha had reached the ninth standard and is now more focused on her studies. In year first term, she scored average marks. She was content with her marks. She even topped her chemistry paper. She was very happy with the fact that her hard work paid off. She scored well in all the subjects except Maths. The only subject that she did not like was Maths.

It was her second term, and she was down with fever. It became so worse that she had to be admitted to hospital. Her condition was very bad, and doctors were trying their level best, but the temperature was not dropping. As days passed, she started to recover but somehow, she missed her second term.

She regretted missing her exams. But everyone tried to console her by saying that should be grateful to God that is alive. Trisha believed in atheism and always had faith that what was happening was happening for good.

Whenever anything happened and Trisha would vouch for why it happened, God would answer her prayers immediately. This time too it happened. The same was her situation when she was admitted to the hospital, and she had to miss her exams. She felt helpless. At the same time, she came to know Aman's friend Debbotam had to miss a year and he could not appear for his tenth standard boards examination. She thanked God for the fact that she was very lucky The Almighty helped her.

After missing a term, Trisha still performed well in her third term. Her overall marks were quite well. She was quite satisfied with her overall marks.

1(v) A New Beginning:

It was her first board exam that is the tenth standard exam. She was always calculative as to how much she would fetch. But this time it was not the same. She was tensed especially in history and maths indeed. She felt that once her history paper was over, she would feel at cloud night. Pooja her sister, would read out the history portions to Trisha. This would make Trisha gasp at the portions that she found difficult to learn and understand.

This was the only time Trisha would become the listener to Pooja. There were more than four people who would be listeners to Trishna, her mature friend Maumita Ganguli, which Trisha called her 'moms.' Pooja her sister, cum secret box, her eldest brother Vikrant and of course her Mummy.

To keep quiet and study was the most different part for Trisha. She can't keep quiet. You won't believe that when there was no one around she would keep talking to herself.

To keep Trisha, cool and calm, Trisha's uncle took all the children to an idly shop for a change. After reaching there, suddenly after a few minutes, Trisha collapsed. Everyone was tense. The uncle sprinkled some water on your face. Trisha felt better and everyone returned home. Everyone was vouched for different analysis of Trisha's falling. But the majority sensed that it was because of stress though Trisha felt it may be so but felt that there was humid also.

Just before her tenth standard exams, she was very stressed. Exams started and the third paper was history. As soon as she completed the history paper she told Maumita that it felt that the tenth standard boards were finished. Trisha was very happy and content. Ultimately all seemed big enough and grown up.

The results were out. In all subjects except Maths Trisha scored above 60. Trisha felt very gloomy about the marks attained in Maths. Whenever someone asked about her, she could first tell her Maths and then other papers.

Trisha recollected her memories of her tenth-standard friends. Some were leaving schools, and some were segregated into science, commerce, and humanities streams. The moment was very sensitive, and it felt as if something new, was to be created. The moment was very touchy. Some eyes were wet, and some hid their emotions to cherish the moment. It's truly said everything comes to an end, but the end also specifies that a new beginning will start soon.

1(vi) Nature:

After two months, standard eleventh standard started. Trisha's tenth-standard students moved to the science stream and 60 percent of the commerce students were admitted from outside. Trisha's nature was to always make friends and be a people's person.

Trisha's soft and sensitive nature was a concern for her family and friends. Once Trisha's father asked "How was your studying going?" She kept numb and felt very bad. She just shook to mean yes. After which Trisha made a notion in her mind that her father thought she was not studying. She started sobbing.

A few moments later, her mother entered the room and saw Trisha sobbing. She immediately enquired as to the fact, what happened? Then Trisha narrated what had happened. Her mother tried to explain to Trisha and told her to be bold and strong. Her mother wanted Trisha to be groomed in such a way that she was completely strong and soft depending on the situation.

2. Simple but Stubborn:

Trisha in her adulthood grew up to be a simple and bubbly girl. Though she was simple and obedient but became stubborn and pampered too. There was an incident where she wanted to get drenched in rain. Her friends asked for an umbrella, she readily gave it. All her friends started saying "You are so obedient then why were you lying" To which Trisha replied "My father told me to carry an umbrella, but he did not tell me to use it. All laugh out loud."

Trisha was becoming stubborn day by day. She would always do and would think that it was only correct. Trisha is an ascetic and wears a locket given by her maternal grandmother and never parted it till date.

Nobody's words matter to her, and she would consider herself supreme to others. She did not realize until a senior boy, a house captain of the school. One day he was monitoring Trisha's class. He was very strict and everyone must listen to whatever she says. Meanwhile, somebody called Trisha, and she looked back. The house captain thought Trisha was talking and told her to go out and stand immediately. Trisha did not get up and started arguing with him that she was not talking and wouldn't go out. After Trisha's denial, the house captain warned her if she did not obey his orders, she had to accompany him to the principal's office. Even after listening to these words, she did not move. The house captain headed to the principal's office. To Trisha's luck, the principal had left for the day. The house captain spoke with Trisha and bluntly told her that she was very stubborn.

Trisha in no time replied if she was right why should she be punished. She explained the whole incident and the house captain understood her point, but he kept his point to Trisha. Trisha agreed to his point too and then they became very good friends.

Trisha started becoming more understanding that there are always two sides to a coin, and everyone can lose or gain. Accordingly has their perspective. Nothing is right or wrong, it is only one's perspective that matters.

2(i) Self-Awareness and Motivation:

With friends from all ages, Trisha enjoyed and cherished everyone's company. But the most she liked was the company of people who were older than her. Most of the seniors were becoming friends were her and with some of them her wavelength matched a lot.

It was the eleventh standard. Aman had tried to make her understand that if she were to prove herself, there was one chance left which was her twelfth standard board exams. Trisha somehow gulped the fact that she was the only one who could help herself. Others can guide the path, but she has to reach her destination on her own. Both brothers Vikrant and Aman were torchbearers for Trisha's path. Vikrant enrolled Trisha in Accounts classes and Aman enrolled her in Maths classes. Enrolment in Maths was the most difficult part because Trisha was weak in Maths, and she needed someone who could give or explain the basics of Maths. She needed someone who could answer the questions from scratch. The maths teacher was one from whom

Aman was preparing for IIT and JEE.

One day, Aman took Trisha to his Maths teacher, Aman showed her interest and intention to guide and teach Maths to Trisha. The teacher tried to explain that he only teaches science streams to IIT and JEE. Moreover, I can't teach a single student. To which, Aman promptly said, if we make a group can you teach? To which sir said OK. So, it was sorted, and the foundation was built. Now Trisha had to mix the cement and pick up and place bricks to stand the best house of her career.

2(ii) Last Two Years of School:

The two years after a tenth that is eleventh and twelfth standard were considered the most crucial years for any student. It was the years where one needs to decide wants, he/she wants to become in life and these two years are also the ones after which no one will help you decide for your decisions in life. Trisha knew if she did not enjoy her last two years, she would regret her whole life.

She was told by her father "Enjoy your days in school because the memories will be with you all your life " All your friends will choose different paths. So, Trisha did all her naughtiness in school and studied at home.

Trisha was a mischievous student, but she was also in the good books of all teachers. Whenever she did some naughtiness, she was never caught. Even if she were caught, she would convince her teachers that she was not involved in it or otherwise. None of her pranks were hurtful, it involved a silly one.

In one of her pranks, she changed her to last bench. She was doing economics in class of Mathematics. One of her classmates made her laugh. She laughed in such a high pitch that the teacher who was teaching facing the board turned. Seeing the teacher turn, Trisha stopped laughing. Again, someone made Trisha laugh and she laughed very loudly. This time the teacher in a fury headed towards the last bench. This time it was sure; Trisha would be completely bowled. One because she was not studying and secondly, she was studying Economics instead of Mathematics. To Trisha's luck, the moment she headed to the last bench, the teacher completely forgot where she was heading. At that very moment, a friend passed her maths notebook. As the teacher went by Trisha was spared.

2(iii) *Took Life Casually:*

Trisha was a person who always played pranks not only with others but always with herself. She also wanted to try and experiment with each and everything in life. In her terms, there is only one life so you or anybody should do everything possible. There were things that she did like crossing the road casually, jumping from a bus, and trying to come between the metro gates. She never understood the real meaning of life.

Her friends always tried to explain and discourage her from doing these odd activities. The one activity changed in her life changed everything. One of Aman's friends met with a bus accident and lost his life. He was trying to get off the bus and another bus came from behind and he died.

That day, she realized that is it the life that matters to your near and dear ones. The person loses his or her life but is the people who are they are the one who are there who must cope to live a life without them.

That day Trisha promised that she would not play or gamble with her life. Trisha's saying that one day everyone must go, so why take stress, just enjoy life. Everyone indeed must go but it does not mean to take your life in your hands.

2(iv) Value of Life:

Now, Trisha understood life better. She understood that you may die but it becomes difficult to live without you for others. One day in school it was announced that we lost a child. There were two minutes of mourn for the student who lost a child. Later she didn't know how he left his life or what had happened to him. It was running in her mind how the student lost his life. The moment she reached home she started to throw questions, "What would have happened to that boy". Her Mother was numb to hear that. She was so shattered about the boy and uttered "May his soul rest in peace". Trisha did not say too much, and she again propelled question

What is life and death? Her mother had no answer to it and neither she wanted to explain to Trisha. She knew Trisha would at this age of fourteen years will not able to understand death and life.

Trisha's mind still had lots of questions, but she didn't know who to ask so she kept quiet.

The two incidents, in front of Trisha, the death of Aman's friend and the student that was lost in the school made her realize that life is a precious gift, which one should cherish and not play with it.

Trisha never crossed the road casually now, got down off the bus or metro very carefully, and did all possible ways to protect the 'LIFE' and it's every moment of it

She understood why her mother kept quiet and knew Trisha would find the answers to them someday.

"Nobody has to pour truth into your brain. It is something you have to find for yourself

- Noam Chowsy"

2(v) Bold and Beautiful:

Trisha had become fearless and didn't entertain any injustice to anybody. In school, one day, a boy named, Manish, was asked for a blade by a girl Jessica.

Manish did not know why she asked for a blade. She had asked to cut her veins. Her brother, Willams, saw it and in a fury slapped Manish. Manish kept quiet because Willams was one of the rowdy students of the class. As Trisha watched this, she couldn't bear it. She immediately went to Willams and asked why he slapped Manish. Willams replied "It was none of her business and she should not get into it" Now the water had reached the brim, and Trisha had lost her temper. All her friends tried to console her but in vain.

She challenged Williams that she would not leave him easily.

"Live for yourself and you will live in vain.
Life for others, and you will live again.
- Bob Marley"

She headed towards the principal office, but he had left his office for the day. It was Friday so Trisha had to wait till Monday. She was bubbling with anger but had no choice.

As Trisha reached home, she narrated the whole incident to her brother, Vikrant. Vikrant told her why she always must come in between others' matters. Then he said, "It is okay, if you can handle it's fine, or else call me I will come." The passing of two days was like the passing of one year. Monday came and the moment Williams saw Trisha, he tried to talk to her. But Trisha was in no mood to talk to him or even look at him. He tried apologizing to Trisha again and again and finally, she gave up. After that, Willams promised that he would not behave badly or rudely with anyone. Till date, I have not found him behaving badly with anyone.

That day a soul had changed for good.

2(vi) Always Do What She Likes:

Trisha was very fond of movies and listening to songs. On weekdays her parents would take them to the cinema halls. Till the end of the 1990s and the beginning of 2000, Walkman was very prevalent. Walkman, a portable audio player, which needed a cassette so that songs could be played. Trisha would listen to music and songs all the long.

Once during her mid-exams, like any Friday, a movie was released. Some of her friends had seen the movie and started praising it. Trisha returned home and showed her interest in seeing the movie. Her mother told her that she will take her to watch the movie once she completes her exams. Aman in a high pitch told Trisha, "You will not see the movie until her exams are over". The moment Aman left the room, Trisha insisted to her mother that if she did not see the movie today, she would not fetch good marks in the exam as her mind would be struck or engrossed about the movie.

Her mother knew very well that if Trisha did not watch the movie today, she would do terribly in the exam the next day. She took her to watch the movie and performed in the exams very well. Aman was very annoyed by the fact that Trisha would always do what she wished to. He was very worried about the fact as to what would happen when something goes against her. Similarly, Vikrant was also concerned about it. Trisha would tell him, "I will always do what I want to." To which Vikrant replied, "In life, sometimes we have to do things that we don't like".

2(vii) Weakness Turning Into Strength:

Amid all these incidents happening in life, Trisha was enjoying her life and making memories and same time studying hard at home. Mathematics had become her favourite subject now. She understood one thing, if you fear and run from something, it becomes more difficult to achieve and understand it. You must love it and keep trying until you achieve it. No subject is good or bad, it is we who create the notion. Twenty-four of the day, her mind kept circulating about maths problems. Even in her dreams, she would think about it. Now her dreams too were captured with Maths problems. Until and unless she solved her Maths sums, her mind would be occupied with those. It's a pronated saying "Try, Try, and try until you succeed."

"A dream is not that which you see while sleeping, it is something that doesn't let you sleep- Dr A.P.J Kalam."

In her first term exams of the eleventh standard, Trisha for the very first time stood ninth in class. She became the talk of the class. Just two months ago, the same Trisha who was feeling low about her attaining 54 in her tenth board exams was now boosting up grooming for performing well in her twelfth board exams.

She felt very proud of herself. But she knew that it was only the first step to success. She must walk a long way.

Trisha loved English Literature, one because of her teacher and secondly because she loved to use proverbs and idioms in her daily life. English was one of the subjects in which she scored marvellously well.

Though Trisha was turning her weakness into reality but her habit of giving up in some way or other still stayed.

3. *Found True Love:*

In between the purpose of Trisha growing bold and beautiful, many boys fell for her. Most of which Trisha hardly knew. She became a beauty with brains. There was a friend of Trisha named Raj who she admired a lot. She knew he didn't have the same feeling as her. She would always say to her mother that she must choose her groom, and she must approve of it. Her mother was always scared of the fact that God knows who she will fall for. Her mother knew about Raj and knew that Trisha had a great crush on him, but he was not the one that she wanted to marry. Trisha deep down knew that she is yet to find her soulmate.

Then among the new students who joined the school, there was one boy who caught her eye. The moment she saw him, something happened inside her and it was love at first sight. She found her soulmate.

She rushed to Maumita as usual and told her about him. She did not even know his name, but she said it was him. After school, he was just walking in front of her. Trisha was with Maumita and in a filmy way Trisha said "If he turns around as I say turn, then he will have the same feeling and they will unite very soon".

To their surprise, the moment Trisha said turn, he turned. Trisha felt as if she was on cloud nine. Trisha and Sunny (the boy Trisha fell for) had no conversation between them. It was a day, when Trisha did not go to school. In the evening, she had her tuition. When she reached the class, one of her friends, asked why she not showed up in school today.

She answered "Just like that, not anything specific"

Pawan took Trisha's notebook and wrote a landline number. He said this was Sunny number and he wanted to talk to her. It would be late when she reached home so she called from an STD booth.

As soon as Trisha called, Sunny picked up the call and asked why she not come to school today, and everything was alright on her side. Trisha replied, "It's strange that I am calling you and why I did not come to school I am only saying?" Sunny stated that he did not have her landline number, so how would he call? This was the beginning of their story. They never felt any friendship between them. They always felt they were soulmates and admired each other a lot.

Now, they talk in school a lot and even on the landline. They talked about a lot of things like cricket, songs, studies and many more things. In school, Trisha would go to his seat beside him and do studies together. They loved each other company.

3(i) Starting a New Chapter:

Sunny was the exact opposite of Trisha. He was shy and an introvert and Trisha was outspoken and an extrovert. Sunny never showed his feelings to Trisha neither did Trisha. Everybody in class could see the chemistry growing between them. Everyone teased them but they did not react to it.

One day, Sunny did not turn up to school. Trisha kept thinking the whole day what would have happened to him. As soon as the school got over, Trisha rushed to the STD booth and dialled his number. She did not even have the patience to reach home and call him.

It was a time when they had to give farewell to their seniors. All the girls decided to wear sarees. Trisha wore a magenta-coloured saree. Trisha didn't know the fact that Sunny had noticed her so closely. Later, when they were getting farewell, Sunny asked, "Will you be wearing that magenta-coloured saree that you wore before?" Trisha herself did not recall that she had worn what Sunny just mentioned. Trisha in a surprised way replied, "You remember what saree I wore when we gave a farewell to the seniors. Sunny did not say a word and tried to keep his eyes away from Trisha. Sunny and Trisha getting close day by day.

4. *Dedication Towards Studies:*

Class twelve boards were about to come. Trisha was very clear and dedicated to the fact that she had to perform her best. She had not forgotten Aman's words that this would be her last chance to prove herself. She also remembered that she had promised her father that she would get admission to the best college. She as usual started evaluating as much she should score in each subject. She knew the number of marks she needed to score to get admission to the best college. Trisha knew her strengths and weaknesses. Mathematics was now become her best scorer subject. She considered this both a strength and a weakness. Strength because whatever she does, she will give 100% of her attention, and her weakness because sometimes to be multitasker .

Trisha never cheated in exams. Rather I would say, she didn't know how to cheat. She believed that if she cheated in exams, she would get lower marks too. She believed in self-development and was an altruist. She did not compare herself with anybody. She only estimated how much she studied and how many marks she would get. Though she looked up to the ones who scored better than her but was never jealous of why they scored more than her.

Once Trisha scored some extra marks in a Hindi exam. She immediately went to the teacher and told her that she by mistake gave her extra marks. The teacher was quite impressed with her. Trisha believed that honesty is the best policy. This quality was imbibed by the father. He would say "Never lie, always be honest".

"A truth can walk naked, but a lie always needs to be dressed.

- Khalil Gibran"

"Of all the liars in the world, the worst are our fears
- Rudyard Kipling"

4(i) Farewell Day:

Trisha and Sunny would talk about studies more than usual. Just a month before the exams, they had their farewell. Girls decided to wear a saree in black coloured and boys in black suit pants. The theme was black and white for the farewell. Though both Trisha and Sunny did not wear black.

Many games were conducted. There was one game in which two people would have to pass a hula loop as many times as possible without dropping the hula loop on the ground. The principal of the school had recommended this game and warned the students not to come in as a couple. They will be at their own risk if they do.

Trisha saw Sunny was not participating in any of the games. Trisha insisted Sunny to play with her. At first, he hesitated but Trisha's continuous request Sunny agreed. The very moment they came to the floor, everyone screamed. The principal boomed, "Oh there is a couple on the floor". Jasleen, one of the students at once clicked a photo and both Trisha and Sunny blushed.

The game started, and Sunny and Trisha couldn't pass the hula loop even once. The hula loop got stuck in Trisha's saree. Sunny did not feel angry that they were out of the game. He tried to remove the hula loop from Trisha's saree. The hula-loop was not just big enough for two people to pass. Trisha in her lifetime met many boys but Sunny was not only different but extraordinary in all aspects. Though Sunny tried to remove the hula loop from Trisha's saree, he kept in mind that he doesn't touch her even by mistake

The farewell ended the same way as all things come to an end. Trisha returned home. As soon as she reached home, she narrated the complete incident to her mother as to how the hula loop struck the saree. She also added that Sunny is the most decent, genuine and gentleman person that she has met in her lifetime. Trisha had a feeling for Sunny but today she also started respecting him.

5. Studying for Exams:

Farewell was over and now it was the time to study for the class twelve boards. Trisha knew that she had to give her best because she had to prove that she had the potential and secondly, this was the last chance to prove to herself that she was not an average student but one of the bright students. Moreover, she had promised her father that she would get admission her father that she will get admission in the best college in Kolkata (Calcutta) (now Kolkata). When Trisha had scored an average in class 10 boards. She felt sad and helpless. That time Aman had consoled her saying that if she performed good marks in her Class twelve board exams then no one would remember her Class 10 results rather she would be judged by her Class results. Aman's words got registered in her head. She used to study in a very systematic way. Though she studied 9 to 10 hours a day neither she did use to get up too early nor study till late at night. Sometimes she would sit back and practice maths at night time as it would be calm and quiet for her to concentrate better. She would go back to bed by 11:30 PM max.

Just one month before her exams, she had been to her maths teacher. Her teacher told her that he doesn't think that she will top in her maths exams among the other students in class. Trisha felt very offended She couldn't understand why suddenly her teacher told those words to her. But she became more than determined to perform her best and not just good.

Trisha's first paper was maths, and she had just a month left for the exams. Just because her maths teacher told her that she would not perform at the top in her tuition, she did all the maths portion again in a month.

5(i) *Offset of School Life:*

Examination day came. Her first paper was Mathematics. Trisha had a habit of not talking to anyone before the exams so that she was calm and composed. The paper went well and Trisha as usual analysed how much she would fetch. She reached home and Aman's friend Vishal opened the door. He asked Trisha "How was the paper?" To his question, she promptly replied, "I will score ninety-two marks." Aman interrupted Trisha, "What's gone is gone. Now study for the rest of the paper. You have only appeared for one paper."

The papers were going well. Until her commerce came. She had great expectations for the commerce paper and even before attempting the paper visualized that she would score ninety-plus marks in it. Just the day before the commerce paper because of her expectation of attaining ninety-plus marks she felt she didn't remember a word. She felt very tense. Though she sat with the book she could not register anything.

When Aman saw Trisha in this state of mind, he told her to go to bed and sleep and rest. He also assured her that she had been studying the whole year, so just studying the day before exams could not tell how she would perform. Trisha went to bed and the next morning she felt better. She had one to two hours left for the exams to start. She calmly revised some portions and gave her paper. After giving the papers, she felt light.

All the papers were done, and the school life was also over. Though students were cheerful that the exams were over but also felt a void of not attending the school ever.

5(ii) *Nostalgic Feeling:*

Trisha did not know what she would do next in life. Most of her friends and classmates had already thought about what they would know in life next. Most of them choose to pursue Chartered Accountancy or Chartered Secretary or both. However, Trisha did not want to pursue any course with her graduation. She knew very well that she would not be able to do two things at the same time. She very well knew that she was not a multitasker. She wanted to perform well in her graduation and then think about other professional and competitive exams.

The results would come in two months. Trisha had no idea what she would do in these two months. She was feeling very restless as to how and what she will do.

Meanwhile, Trisha missed school badly and the most she missed was Sunny. She conveyed her feelings for Sunny to Vikrant. Vikrant, like always, did not get angry or lose his temper. He simply asked "Did you not tell your feelings for him or whether he has the same feelings as well? To this, Trisha replied that she has never expressed her liking to Sunny and neither he has told anything to her about this". Trisha further added that though none of us had expressed their liking for each other they knew both had a soft corner. The very first time that she looked at him, she knew he was her soulmate. They never became friends. We generally hear that you first became friends and then soulmates. It was not the case with Sunny and Trisha.

5(iii) Reading Habit:

As days passed, she felt very bored and did not know how to spend these two months. She usually visited her aunt's place. One day, Pooja took her to her English teacher's home. On reaching there, the teacher asked Trisha what do you do in your leisure time? Do you read books? There was a small library at her house. Trisha replied "Till now I have only read my course books, and I can't understand how people read novels. I can't study more than two pages and if I do, I will fall asleep."

Pooja's teacher asked, "What type of stories do you like?" I like romantic, thriller and ghost stories. She handed a book of 'Goosebumps' which was a horror thriller to Trisha. Trisha was very sure she would never complete the book. On the teacher's recommendation, she took the book as her respect for her. The teacher assured Trisha that one day she would surely become an avid reader. She also stated that "Books are the best friend of our life, and each book has a story to tell"

Trisha started to read she could hardly one or two pages at a time. But she continued to read slowly. As Trisha always says, "Slow and steady wins the race."

She knew that she had always been slow at learning but once she grasps the art, she will be best at it. Trisha could not believe that she had completed the book. She along with Pooja visited her teacher, Mrs. Mala, the English teacher at her place. This time, she was handed a romantic book by 'Mills and Boon'. She started reading it. Trisha could not part with it. She accompanied the book at all places be it by metro, bus, or at home. It became just like meditation for her. One day Aman noticed that Trisha's reading was taking most of her time there. One day Trisha was reading a thriller book and she slept at 3 a.m. Aman noticed Trisha and the next day told her "Excess of everything is bad. You should read the novels in your leisure time rather than reading them at a stretch."

6. Going Apart:

Trisha and Sunny do not talk now. Trisha suddenly noticed that Sunny was not ready to talk to her. She tried to ask him "Why aren't you not talking to me?" But he said nothing and rather told Trisha to make out the reason for his ignorance. Trisha was the only girl he ever spoke to or made any forget about speaking to any other girl. Trisha was the exact opposite. She hardly had any friends who were girls, and she would have all the friends who were boys. Trisha used to mingle with people with people very easily, so she was adored by all. Maybe this was the reason; Sunny was not talking to her or something else. She couldn't figure it out at all.

Two months passed by, and the results were out. Unlike today, in yesterday's time marks were struck on billboards and students visited their school to look at their marks fetched. All the students gathered at school to check the results. Trisha was very content with the marks she scored. When she looked at Sunny's marks, it was the same as her marks. Though they were not on talking terms, they did not say anything. But all the other students were comparing each other marks. They were saying "Both Trisha and Sunny had scored the same percentage".

If you remove the name, you will not come to know whose marks, is it.

Jasleen, the girl who clicked the photo on farewell day handed the photo to Trisha. Trisha glanced at the photo and sweet memories flashed over her eyes. She felt a belonging was achieved and that she would always keep it as a treasure which would be a rare and priceless gift.

6(i) *The Outcome of Results:*

Everyone was proud of Trisha at home. They had not imagined that she would pass her twelfth board with flying colours. Everyone started to ask what her plans are. What does she plan to pursue? At that very moment, Trisha's only aim was to get admission to the college her father had always wished for.

Meanwhile, all her friends were planning to pursue professional and completive exams with graduation. Her accounts tuition friend, Ankit, called her and tried to convince Trisha to enrol in the professional exams and they were going to get to the forms. Trisha promptly said, "I can't do a course with my graduation as of now." He still tried but Trisha was firm in her decision.

Trisha got admission to the college her father always dreamt of. Trisha was very happy not because she got admission to the best of the college but most importantly because gave her father the happiness, he always wanted all these years.

Though Trisha and Sunny had a long time, that they were talking, Sunny was always there in Trisha's thoughts. One day, Trisha felt in her subconscious mind that she would meet Sunny today. Aman got admitted to NIT (now Kozhikode) so he needed to go shopping. Aman and shopping can never go together just like tracks and trains. First, he hated shopping and secondly, if he needed anything, Vikrant was also there for him. Most of the family members were going shopping, even, Trisha was. But the telepathy of meeting Sunny circled in her mind. At one time she would say yes and another moment no. At last, she went.

6(ii) Encounter with Sunny:

Trisha with her family members reached the shopping mall. She was looking for some T-shirts for Aman. In between the stack of T-shirts, she sensed it was Sunny with her classmate Vishal. The very moment her heart started beating rapidly.

She was 200% sure that her telepathy or intuition always worked. Trisha's mother took Trisha casually and told her, "They may be someone else. Just because you were thinking about him so deeply, you are finding him all around yourself, you must have visualized someone as him." Trisha closed her tightly and then opened her eyes. She was correct, it was Sunny. Trisha did not digest the fact it was him. Just they were still not on talking terms, so they did not talk. Their eyes met and that's all. She thought if she could have wished for anything else today, it would have become true today. Trisha was admiring him without him getting noticed by her. She would peek in between the stack of clothes, sometimes from right and sometimes from left at him. Trisha was dying to talk to him but did not make any move towards him.

Trisha knew that if Sunny were not ready to talk to her, nobody could dare convince him. Shopping was over and all the members were standing for Vikrant to pay the bill. At that moment, Vishal came over and started talking to Aman. Aman did not recognize Vishal. Vishal commented "Hello bhaiya, I am Vikash's brother who studies with you" Aman nodded his head, and they had one or two minutes of conversation between them. Trisha introduced Sunny to everyone and Vishal as well. Trisha desperately wanted to talk to Sunny, but he was numb. Trisha said bye and left.

Trisha was leaving for home, but she did not want to. She wished that she could just be there and admire Sunny all her life. But it was just a dream that she was looking at her with open eyes. Dreams that people see with their eyes closed seldom become true and here she was seeing something with her naked eyes.

6(iii) A New Road:

Finally, college was about to resume. Trisha along with Vikrant went to pay the admission fees. Vikrant handed the fee amount to Trisha and told her to enrol in the college. As Trisha was proceeding to pay, Vikrant interrupted "Don't argue with anyone, just pay and come." Vikrant knew Trisha very well, if she found anything wrong or against her, she would not keep quiet and speak for it.

Trisha was standing in a queue to submit the admission fees. After some time realized that the line was not moving. She had been standing in one place for quite a long time. Students were breaking the line or allowing their friends to join in between. She could not bear it. She ran towards the counter and expressed her view. The person at the counter was neither ready to hear nor pay any heed to Trisha's saying. But Trisha was not a person who would just let it go.

At last, the person at the counter himself witnessed how the queue was moving and acted. The girls in a queue were taken aback by the courageous act of Trisha. Trisha paid her fees and went to Vikrant. Vikrant asked, "What took you so long?" To which Trisha answered and explained every bit of what had happened. Vikrant patiently listened to Trisha. He recalled the words that he told Trisha. He then said, "I told you not to argue or be stubborn." To Vikrant's words, Trisha just nodded her head and kept quiet.

Trisha was the only girl from her school who had been admitted other than two more. Trisha was hardly in touch with them, and they were in different sections, so Trisha had no connection with them. The college started and the first day when she entered the classroom, she found herself lost.

Firstly, because there were approximately two hundred and fifty girls in the class, and she had never seen so many girls in one place. She could not bear the chit-chat of those girls. You very well know how much Trisha gel up with girls or have a wavelength with them. Isn't it? She ran out of the classroom.

7. *Adjusting to Situations:*

One day, Trisha's father asked her, "How is your college going?" Trisha prompted, "Papaji I don't know how I will study in a class that only consists of two hundred and fifty girls. To which her father replied "Just because you have studied in a co-education class till twelfth standard, you are saying this. Give some time to yourself, you will be fine."

Though, Trisha listened to her father's words but for a week she did not enter the class. As it is truly said, "There is always a first time for all things". Trisha had to begin her new life in the college, and she knew very well that there was no choice, it would be better for her to accept and start afresh.

After one week, Trisha at last entered the class. She loved to sit at the last bench. She chose the last bench because she always had to sit on the first bench in school. She turned and a girl named Shweta said, "Aren't you Trisha, the girl who raised her voice on the day of paying the admission fees." To which Trisha nodded her head in affirmation.

As days passed by, Trisha started to adjust to the circumstances of college life. She managed to make three who were less girl-like. I mean they were somewhat like Trisha and the wavelength matched between them.

7(i) New Friends:

Trisha was talking with a friend on the landline when there was a call waiting buzz. She kept the call on hold and took the other call. Guess, who was on the line? You are right. It was Sunny. Trisha was very delighted to hear his voice but got scared at the same time. She told Sunny "Please don't call on the landline?" But then, how would they talk? Trisha told him that she would call him when she wanted to.

Trisha joined tuition at the start of the first year. It was not that the teachers at her college were not good. The only reason for taking was to be in touch with her studies. Unlike school, college was a free bird. There would be no one who would tell you to study. There would be no one who would tell you to study or attend classes regularly. So basically, you are expected to make your decisions and perform well.

Trisha arrived late on the first day of tuition. As she entered, all of them prompted to the teacher that as per the rules of the class, the person who comes late must sing. The teacher looked at Trisha and told her to sing a song. Trisha sang her heart out and everyone loved it. Then all of them applauded and said, "There is no such rule". Trisha made new sets of friends in the tuition class who were in the same college as her.

8. The First Meeting:

Trisha's life was getting into tracks once again. She made more friends, and their wavelength matched. Luckily, some of the friends in the tuitions were from her college. So now she liked girls more than usual. Her myth of making friends who were girls vanished. Sunny and Trisha started to talk very frequently, the calls became daily, and gradually a time came when the calls increased to more than 4-5 calls a day. They only talked on the phone. Both wanted to meet. So, one day they decided to meet. Trisha accompanied her friend, Rupal to meet him.

They fixed a place to meet. Neither Trisha nor Sunny had a mobile phone. It was a time when mobile phones were not as prevalent as today. Trisha was desperately waiting to see Sunny and vice-versa. But there was no sign of him. Rupal sighed, "Why don't you get a cell phone"?

Trisha went to a nearby STD booth and called Sunny's place to check whether he had left. No one picked so she understood he had left from his home.

Suddenly, Trisha got a glance at Sunny. That moment was priceless. Both just looked at each other without saying a word. They went to the temple together and time slipped like seconds. They were a time to depart and say goodbye to each other.

Trisha and Rupal boarded a bus heading home. Sunny too boarded. Trisha asked "Where are you going? To which Sunny replied, "Can I drop you home?"

There were very few passengers on the bus. Trisha and Sunny were continuously staring at each other.

Their eyes met. Trisha withdrew her eyes in shyness. Sunny said, "It's been ages since we met." Let me look at you. Time flew and Trisha reached home hoping when they would see each other soon.

8(i) Love Above Everything:

The exams of the first year went well. Now it was time for the second-year exams. Both Sunny and Trisha did talk daily but they also concentrated on their studies. The second-year exams were approaching, and they scored well. Now only final exams were left for their graduation. Sunny had taken two professional courses along with graduation with the bachelor's degree. He had cleared his foundation, that is, the first level of both courses. At the mid-year, his second level for the Company Secretaries of India was due. For the first paper, Sunny left, the examination centre thirty minutes ago. He called Trisha and requested her to meet. Trisha was shocked at his call. Trisha asked her mother, "Mummy can I please go and meet Sunny, it's urgent." Her mom neither said no nor yes. Trisha requested her mother and convinced her that she would come back as soon as possible.

As soon as Trisha met Sunny, she started yelling at him. She said, "How come you completed the paper half an hour?" I hope you did not do this so that we could meet. Sunny completely denied the allegation. But he only knew why it happened.

"*Love comes naturally. Hate is taught.*
- Nelson Mandela"

8(ii) Only Trisha:

Sunny got a desktop at home. He started writing emails to Trisha. The thoughts that were not spoken has now been expressed via mail. He wrote to Trisha very frequently unlike Trisha. Trisha loved reading his emails. It would make her feel so special. He would always say, "I am a liability, and you are an asset, isn't it?" Vikrant gifted a cell phone to Trisha on her birthday. I don't know whether it turned out to be a blessing or a curse. Now Trisha would call Sunny when she wished to, and Sunny would do the same. There were no restrictions at all on both ways. After a month, the telephone bill of Sunny was five thousand rupees, and his most dialled number was Trisha's. Though Trisha felt bad, they did not stop talking. They divided the number of calls among themselves. Sunny just could not concentrate on his studies. Though he did not admit. Everyone could see it very well. Trisha was in his mind 24*7. If Trisha called and at that very moment he was studying, he would keep talking and give preference to Trisha's call. It happened most of the time.

8(iii) Sweet Moments:

Sunny and Trisha did not realize that there was not a single day when they would not talk to each other. They became obsessed with each other as bread and butter. One day while talking on the phone, Sunny expressed his love for her. Trisha kept silent and did not say a word. Days passed and then after one week

Sunny said, "You did not say anything when I spoke my heart out." Finally, after a week she said those magical words, Sunny had always dreamt of.

On the Rose Day, which falls on 7th February every year, Trisha wanted to surprise Sunny by giving him roses. She did not know how. Just because exams were nearing, they did not want to be distracted. Sunny had once told her where his mother worked. But she did not know the name. Immediately she called and asked Sunny's brother what was the name of Aunty. She said thank you and hung up the phone. When Trisha came across Sunny's mother, she handed the economics notes to her and requested her to have the notes to Sunny. Sunny's mother asked, "Are you Trisha?" She replied "Yes." Then she handed a small packet and told her to give this to Sunny as well.

On reaching home, Sunny took the notes and opened the small packet in front of everyone. There were two red roses in it. He blushed and left without saying a word. Then he called Trisha and said, "Are you crazy?" Trisha responded, "I wanted to give roses to you, and I found this the best way." Trisha said, "Why did you open it in front of everyone?" To which he replied, "How will I ever imagine that there will be roses in it?" Sunny simply loved the way of expressing her admiration for him.

After a week on the 14th of February that is on Valentine's Day, Sunny made great plans and wanted to spend the day with Trisha. Trisha denied. Sunny felt very angry and wanted to know what the reason besides not meeting. Sunny felt whenever she wanted to meet or talk, he was always available. Only when he says, Trisha would always say no whatever the reason behind it. They would hardly meet, and it was the 14th of February, so Sunny wanted to meet.

They finally did not meet but Trisha was very confident that she would make sure that Sunny understood her viewpoint. Sunny understood her point of view and wrote a mail expressing that this incident had brought them closer. Now he respects and adores her more than before.

8(iv) *The Final Phase of College Life:*

The final year of college was about to commence in one and a half months. Sunny had to get some notes from Trisha. Trisha was busy and could not make it. She called him near the tuition centre to collect the notes. Sunny reached to collect the notes. He was very emotional that day though he was always, when wherever they met. He suddenly said, "Don't ever leave me, I want to spend my entire life with you." Trisha said, "I will never spend my life without you too."

Sunny went home and Trisha headed to her tuitions. It was almost twenty days left for the exams. Trisha always preferred self-study but this time for a change she was doing her practical subjects with her friends. Preparations were going well. Once again like the twelfth board exams, Sunny and Trisha discussed what they studied and cleared their doubts.

Exam started. As usual, Trisha set a benchmark for how much marks she should get in each paper even before she attempted the paper. All papers were good except Mathematics. At the time of writing the Maths paper, she realized the paper was a walk in the park. She made it a point that she got no less than

90%. This made her overconfident and nervous, so she scored less than she expected. Somehow, she finished writing her paper. She was very vexed with herself. But there was no point regretting it now. Sunny called and asked, "How was your paper?" Trisha narrated what had happened at the examination hall. When Sunny heard this, he responded, "You won't believe that I felt something is wrong with you." Take care of yourself and we will meet after all the papers are over.

9. The Goal:

Finally, exams were over. Everyone was happy about the fact all the papers were over. Trisha was the only one who was not happy. She was worried about what she would do from tomorrow. The very thought of being ideal made her restless. That day, she met Sunny and expressed of pursuing an MBA

Trisha said the same thing to Vikrant. After looking into all the pros and cons, Vikrant expressed his opinion. He told Trisha, "If she gets his admission in B- school then only she will be allowed to go." Trisha understood what Vikrant was trying to say. But the question remained the same as to what she should pursue. Vikrant suggested pursuing a Chartered Accountancy course. Chartered Accountancy was one of the toughest courses and it was not her cup of tea. Trisha said, "I will think about it and let you know?" After giving it a thought, she decided to do Chartered Accountancy.

When Trisha spoke to Sunny and expressed her view of pursuing CA, he was left with words. He said,

"I thought you wanted to do an MBA and not a CA." Can't you make your decisions?" Trisha tried to tell Sunny why she was taking CA. It was not because of Vikrant's suggestion but it was hers. After a discussion with Vikrant, she made up her mind. Vikrant had never pushed her what she should do. CA or MBA eventually would be her call.

9(i) Who Is Lucky?

Final year examination results were out. Trisha scored fairly and Sunny too. There was only one paper in which she felt she secured fewer marks. She was very confident that if she gave her paper for re-valuation, her marks would certainly increase.

Trisha always found Sunny to be lucky. She took Sunny to Calcutta University to submit her re-valuation paper. After a few days, a letter came from Calcutta University stating that there was a change of marks for the re-valuation paper. They reached and the first name that was called was Trisha. The revised marksheet was handed to her and eight marks were increased. She felt joyous and content. She felt that though she was expecting above eighty but seventy-five was also good enough. Now that she had decided to pursue a CA course, she wanted Sunny to submit her enrolment form. Trisha went to the bank to make a demand draft. After she received the demand draft, she headed to the Institute with Sunny. The enrolment form was submitted, and the exams would commence next year.

Since Trisha had scored more than fifty percent in her graduation course, so she was directly eligible for the second level of the CA course.

Sunny had appeared for the second level just after the graduation exams. Trisha did not doubt that she would clear the exam. Sunny's results were out and to his surprise, he had not cleared a single group. When Trisha heard this, she wanted to meet him. Sunny did not utter a word when they met. All of Trisha's efforts to make Sunny speak did not work. Somehow, Trisha felt that it was all her fault. Vishal, a common friend, of Trisha and Sunny told Trisha that it was because of her that Sunny was getting distracted and could not concentrate on his goal of becoming a CA and a Company Secretary.

9(ii) *Focusing on the Goal:*

After accepting the fact that he couldn't clear his exams, he spoke to Trisha. Trisha in a very low and regretted way said, "I am the reason for your failure" Sunny said; "It is rubbish. Did I ever tell you that you are the reason for me not clearing my exams?" She said, "Everyone around is saying this and now I have started to believe." Sunny in a convincing manner said, "The next time I take my exams the results will be positive."

Though Trisha heard Sunny's words she knew very well; she was only the reason for the diversion of his studies. She also knew he would not, even his dreams admit the fact that Trisha is the reason for derailing him from his goal and purpose in life.

Trisha started to study for her exams which were due in ten months. She did not find to take any coaching tuition for the exams. Mostly all the subjects were very familiar to her as the papers that were there in her final stage. At Vikrant's suggestion, Trisha agreed to take tuition for the practical papers. He agreed as there would be a flow, and she would not be diverted from preparing for her exams. Trisha enrolled and kept herself updated on the practical portion. Now, the only concern was the theory papers which she had to take her on her own.

10. Love Not Expressed Is Unheard:

Sunny and Trisha will not meet often, though they talk daily. They both started to have some misunderstandings between them. They could not find a concentrate reason as to why this was happening. It was Sunny's birthday and Trisha wanted to meet him, but he was not quite sure if he wanted to meet. Somehow Trisha convinced him, and they met outside a temple that both used to visit.

Trisha wished him well and handed a packet to him. He asked, "What is inside this?" To which she replied, "It is your birthday gift." He refused to accept and left. Trisha was very keen that she would give him the gift. Trisha had once asked where he lived. She had no idea of the location and its whereabouts. Sunny had mentioned the name of the cinema hall which was his house. It became the landmark for Trisha to reach Sunny. She made it a point she would not move until she reached that place.

She started walking, walking, and walking. She did not know where her journey was. She only knew about her destination. Asking people about the way she headed. Some would say yes and some no. But the stubbornness to meet Sunny and hand over the gift was good enough.

She did not take any mode of commuting because she did not know where she had to go. She only knew that she had to reach the cinema hall and then the rest was easy to find the way to Sunny's home. Trisha must have walked 1.5 hours and finally, she got a glimpse of the hall. She sighed; she did not feel she had walked so long. She only knew she would meet Sunny and hand over the gift to him by hook or by crook. As she reached his complex, the security guard asked the block and the flat no. but she had no clue about it at all. She dialled Sunny at his landline number and said, "I am at you're in your complex. Can you tell me your block and flat, no?" He said, "Wait a minute I will be right there" They went directly to the terrace. He said, "Why are you here?" She said, "Please accept your gift. I can't take it back." Sunny said, "But why? Trisha why don't you understand, I have priorities, and you are not my priority at present." He was so frustrated that he said, "I don't know what to do. I shouldn't live, there will be no more problems than ever." Trisha just could not believe he had spoken these words. She said, "Are you crazy?"

"Suicide is a permanent solution to the temporary problem.
-Shiv Khera"

Never think about this ever. Sunny knew Trisha would not come to his home, so he took her to the terrace. He asked, "Will you come to my place?" To which she said "Yes" They headed. She moved her hand, and she gave the birthday gift. This time did not say no. It was getting late, and she decided to leave. Sunny said, "Mom is about to come". Why don't you wait and meet her? She said, "It's late, I should leave." Sunny went downstairs to see her off.

As they were walking towards the bus stop, Trisha stopped. She came closer to him and asked, "Can you hug me please?". Sunny put his hands behind him and did not hug. Trisha left and boarded the bus. After an hour,

Sunny called to ask, "Did you reach your home?" Trisha replied, "Do you care?"

10(i) *The Best Birthday Ever:*

The next day, Sunny and Trisha talked as if nothing had happened the previous day. The daily talks were on but there was a feeling of dissatisfaction somewhere that troubled both.

Things were getting normal. It was Trisha's birthday. Sunny called at midnight to wish her. They talked and talked. Both did not realize it was 3:00 AM. After talking for around three and a half hours, they wanted to talk more but they hung the call. Around noon, Sunny called Trisha to meet. She sensed he must have been giving a gift and excuse that she would not make it. The only reason was what she would say at home. She did not want to break the trust of her family members. The other reason was Sunny was preparing for his MBA exams and Trisha did not want to distract him at any cost. Trisha with her friends have planned to have lunch together. The moment she entered the metro station, she saw Sunny.

This was the best gift ever. He handed the gift and the boutique to Trisha. Everyone had lunch together. All headed home except Sunny and Trisha. They went to a fair which was supposed to have the last day. They had the best time together. Both loved each other's company, and they did not realize it was eight thirty in the night. They planned to leave for home. This is a birthday as if she reached heaven. Though Trisha's birthday was always celebrated with her near and dear ones. Sunny added the icing on the cake.

11. Trisha's Sudden Fall:

Celebrations were done and now it was time to move on with the normal routine. Trisha's exams were due in five months. She was preparing for it sincerely. One of her close friends, Swapna, got engaged and was about to get married. Trisha went to her marriage and suddenly Trisha fell on the ground. A crowd gathered around her and after a few seconds, she gained consciousness as if nothing had happened. She felt fine. But everyone present, recommended to go to the room and rest for a while. After some time, she came and enjoyed the marriage celebrations. After the marriage was over, Swapna's brother, Pankaj, made a point to drop Swapna's friends to their homes. Till now, Trisha was behaving normal. But the moment she reached home, she fell on her father's feet and started sobbing. Her father was half asleep as it was late at night. As he realized Trisha's voice and the feel of her hand, he was awake. The moment Trisha saw her father move; she started crying uncontrollably. What's wrong? Trisha's father sighed. She narrated the incident at the marriage. Trisha stops sobbing and goes to bed. Though Trisha on obeying her father's word, did go the room but she couldn't sleep.

Trisha needed to resume her studies but somehow, she was not able to. Her mind was preoccupied by the fact of her fall. She found no answers to her questions.

11(i) Sunny's Concern for Trisha:

Sunny heard about Trisha's fall at her friend's marriage. Sunny called Trisha and wanted to meet her. They met. Sunny asked, "Is everything fine with you? Take care of your health." Saying this he left.

After a few said, Trisha started to lose weight and looked very skinny. There was no major issue in Trisha's health but to be sure her parent on the doctor's suggestion conducted some tests. All the tests were completely fine. The doctor did not find any reason for the test conducted.

Trisha 's parents were very worried by this time. Trisha came to Sunny and suggested to Trisha, "Forget about Sunny and concentrate only on your life. Become something in life and let the future be decided by the Almighty." Trisha listened to her father's words but could not forget Sunny. She madly admires Sunny and does not forget him regardless of her father's advice. Sunny called Trisha and enquired about the tests. Trisha signed. She replied that all tests had no issue but why was she losing weight she didn't know and the doctor himself couldn't make out.

He was himself concerned about Trisha but felt helpless.

Sunny and Trisha's relationship was going unstable. After a few days, Sunny called, "Let us meet?" Trisha had to go to Swapna's marriage that day, so they decided to meet the next day. Trisha and Sunny met. Trisha harshly said, "This is our last meeting, we will not talk or meet after this." Sunny insisted, "We can be friends at least?" Trisha very well knew that they could never be friends, they were soulmates and would always be. They parted ways. They did not know what fate had in store for them. Trisha always thought that if something adverse happened, she would be able to cope with it. But she knew Sunny would not be able to overcome it.

It has happened in the past that Sunny had told Trisha, if we can't live together at least we can die together. In another incident, during one of their meetings, Sunny in a state of frustration told Trisha," It is better if I take my life." Trisha knew Sunny had a lot of responsibilities towards his family as well. She would never want Sunny to even think about taking his life ever and anyone for that matter.

11(ii) Last Meeting:

At their last meeting, Sunny told Trisha, "We are too young to commit to each other now. We should both concentrate on our studies and build a career." Trisha in a gullible way responded, "We can get married and study together". Sunny answered, "I am not settled now neither are you, nor how will"

I take your responsibilities. "Give me at least five years to prove myself and then get settled." Sunny pronounced that his priority is not her now. Trisha got offended and asked if her parents someday asked him for her, would he accept or say no if her parents found another match for her, then what would she say? Trisha misunderstood Sunny when he said that his priority was not her now. But Trisha just wanted to know, if he was committed to her.

Trisha understood one thing that in the coming years, there is no certainty what will happen. So, she thought it was better not to go ahead as of now. She knew that she was doing the worst thing ever. But perhaps she had no choice. By doing this she would destroy his personal life however his professional life would be intact. Trisha had always assumed that just because she was the eldest girl child in the joint family, she would be married off early. Though no one ever told her so. This was their last meeting. They turned and never looked back. Words once spoken, can't be taken back. They may be forgiven but not forgotten.

11(iii) *Trisha 'S Guilt for Sunny:*

Though Trisha bluntly told Sunny not to meet or call her ever, she couldn't survive without meeting or hearing his voice. She called Sunny many a time, but he did not response. This time Sunny was determined not to talk or meet Trisha.

She was gloomy because there was not a single day when she didn't meet or hear his voice.

Slowly, Trisha's behaviour started to change. A girl who always spoke and was so bubbly lost all her charm. Gradually, she became more and more silent. Her presence was hardly felt. One day she asked her father, "What's wrong with me?" Her father had no answers for her because he didn't know what was wrong with her.

She visited two or three doctors but just couldn't make out what was happening to her. Everyone in the house became more and more worried about Trisha's health. If doctors did not know what was happening, how would they know what was happening inside her? A day came when Trisha stopped talking at all. She would just lay down on the bed with her eyes open. Neither did she eat nor drink anything. She lost the very essence of being alive. She was breathing or I should just inhale and exhale without feeling it. Trisha's friend, Rupal, would write 'Ram Ram' on Trisha's forehead. Trisha could sense somebody writing 'Ram Ram' on her on her forehand. Many friends would come to Trisha's place and feel very helpless and sad about her.

After about seven days, Trisha uttered the word, "MAA". Maa is a word that mostly a child speaks when he/she is born. It was the same with Trisha, after a span of so much time, she spoke. Everyone was delighted. The expression on her mother was priceless.

Trisha's uncle recommended a doctor. Trisha with her parents and Vikrant went to the doctor. The doctor spoke to Trisha for a while and told her she was in severe depression. In those days, mental health was not talked about as of now. Just like physical illness, mental health is to be treated. This was not known.

There was a sense of relief on the face of all the family members. Now at least they knew what's the cause of Trisha's illness and were sure that Trisha would be cured very soon.

11(iv) *Coming Back to Life:*

The first time she visited the doctor, she weighed forty-five kgs. After one week, she again went to the doctor, and she weighed 48kgs. Though Trisha always would make herself very conscious even at the increase of one kg but this time she had no problems because the situation was different. The doctor prescribed medicines for a month. After a month, her weight was fifty-seven kgs. The doctor jokingly asked, "Did you eat elephant's baby?" Trisha was shocked to hear her weight but what mattered was her health now, everything was baseless at present.

Trisha was recovering at a good pace and getting back to her normal life. Aman returned after completing his Bachelor of Technology degree. The moment he saw Trisha, he was taken aback. He couldn't see his sister, Trisha, in the girl standing in front of him. Vikrant with other family members tried to console him. Aman was very angry because no one ever mentioned about Trisha's health. He felt like a stranger in his own home. Vikrant spoke and tried to explain to Aman that it was his final semester and if he came to know about Trisha, he would certainly leave his exams and come home.

Aman felt very bad about the fact that he was not there with the family members during this tough time. He made it a point that he would spend more and more time with Trisha and help her life on track as usual. They played lots of board games together. One day all the children went to a water park. This was the first time she ventured out of her home. She was very overwhelmed. Everyone enjoyed all types of water games. Trisha enjoyed it as well. Trisha jumped into a pool of water and was not able to come out of it because of her increased weight. Aman as usual shouted, "Come out of the water there is hardly any height in it," Aman didn't want Trisha to be dependent at all and he knew one person who motivated Trisha was only him.

At that moment, Vikrant came and helped Trisha come out of the water. Vikrant stated, "Aman Trisha has to cope with her increased weight and so I helped her out." Both brothers' intentions were always the same that is to help face all hurdles of life and how to deal with them and overcome any fear faced in life.

Trisha's Chartered Accountancy exams were due at this time. She was not able to appear for exams because she had just begun to recover and could not take a chance of taking any stress. Though Trisha did not appear this time, but she made it a point that she would bounce back in the next time. Trisha, along with her father used to visit, mostly in a month. At the next visit, when Trisha went to the doctor, the doctor asked, "What do you want to do in your life now?" Trisha immediately answered, "I want to study further and give my Chartered Accountancy."

The doctor was delighted to hear this from Trisha. Trisha's goal of life was again back in her life. Trisha's doctor could see the curiosity and determination in Trisha's eyes while she spoke. The doctor said, "Trisha just gives your best and keep up the motivation alive until you achieve your ultimate goal." These words were enough to give wings to Trisha's dreams and she was ready to fly.

Sunny was always in Trisha's subconscious mind. All the moments spent with him were fresh in her mind. The only difference was she could not see and hear his voice. They had not spoken after Trisha's illness.

Sunny appeared for his Intermediate level of CA and final level of CS exams. She would know this from the common friends. The same year, Sunny cleared his CS and became a CS and completed his second level and was due for the final level of CA exams. She could not resist to talk to Sunny. In July, she called Sunny on his landline number to congratulate him. He picked up the call and uttered, "Hello." Trisha felt so satisfied to hear Sunny in her voice after such a long time. Trisha in excitement said, "Congratulations!" Sunny did not say a word, but he hung up. Again, when he became a CS, she was very satisfied and felt as if she achieved something. She again calls his number, and he just as before does not say a word.

Trisha felt sad that Sunny did not talk to her but then she recalled her spoken words at their last meeting. She consoled herself by remembering those words and did not feel sad.

12. *Was It Self-Motivation?*

Trisha had to appear for her exams in November the same year as Sunny. She gathered all her self-motivation, perseverance, and support from her family and friends and started to see her dreams with open eyes. Time flew in a blink of an eye and the exams were knocking at the door.

Trisha had enrolled for both the groups and each group had three papers. After appearing for two papers, she could not give her third paper. She was completely ready to go to the examination hall but at that very moment, she started to feel very sleepy. Her father would accompany her to the examination hall. As Trisha told her father, "Papaji, I am feeling very drowsy. I don't think I will be able to take my exam today." Trisha's father, a very positive person, assured Trisha, "Be positive. Give your best and rest leave it to God." He went downstairs to get a taxi. By the time he returned, Trisha had fallen asleep.

When she got up, she felt very sad that she could not go to write her paper. Now the next attempt will take place after six months. After some remorse and frustration, she again rose and headed towards fulfilling her goal. This time too Trisha received all the support and motivation from her family and her doctor. Everyone believed that Trisha would certainly make it one day.

12(i) Finding Oneself:

The confidence and support from her loved ones brought back Trisha's self-motivation and she knew that she would achieve her goal no matter what. She started her journey from scratch to reach her destination. This time she tried to give her 200%.

Six months passed in the blink of an eye. This time, the papers attempted were better than the previous attempt. This time she did smart study rather than hard study because she understood that these are professional courses and not school or bachelor's degree. She appeared for both groups and there was one paper she was doubtful about which was, "Information Technology" which was a paper in which mostly difficult to clear. Trisha as usual, calculated her marks after attempting all the papers. Other students joked as to how she could calculate her marks in competitive or professional exams as in school. But she believed only and solely upon working hard. She believed that we should always compare what we studied and how she fetched the according to her preparation. She said, "If you work with sincerity and perseverance no one can beat you" When Trisha did not clear her second group of the second level of CA exams, she felt bad but as usual she bounced back. This for the first in her life she ever failed an exam. But her principle for life was the same, "If you don't work hard or study smartly, then be it any exam or situation in life you will never fail." She made up her mind and started from scratch. She knew her weakness and strength just like water that is crystal clear which means completely transparent.

In the next exam, she knew where she scored maximum. In the group, there were two practical papers so it was different to predict how much she could achieve. But for the one theory paper, she can put all the efforts as much as possible. This was the same paper because of which she had not cleared her second group. She made sure she would work harder and harder so that this time there was no question of failing. Trisha used to write all the answers after learning it. She made no stone unmoved.

The time for exams came. Trisha was ready to knock the exams just as a boxer knocks out an opponent in the boxing ring. The first paper went so and so. Trisha did not bother because two more papers were left. This was the paper which was difficult paper and other papers were like a walk in the park. The second exam was the 'Taxation' paper. Trisha had prepared Taxation from the book of an author, T.N. Manoharan. This book was recommended by Vikrant. Trisha had brushed all the concepts plus revised every problem in it. She trusted Vikrant like a ray of light in a dark room.

12(ii) A Step Up in Life:

The second paper was "Taxation" and it went well. The third and the last paper was the theory paper of Information Technology paper, which she had her heart and soul in it. The last paper was about what to do and what to leave. She knew all the answers. The third paper went well. At the end of all the papers, Trisha's mother came to pick her up. She said, "How was your paper ?" She confidently said, "I will get sixty-eight out of a hundred marks." She felt very happy about how much she would fetch. Trisha was quite sure she would clear her second level with flying colours. She got almost the similar marks that she had evaluated. In the first paper, she scored forty out of a hundred marks. In the 'Taxation' paper, she scored fifty-six out of a hundred marks and lastly in the Information Technology paper, she scored seventy-three out of a hundred marks. In total, she scored a hundred and sixty-nine marks out of three hundred marks. Now she partly became a Chartered Accountant. No one could believe how she passed her second level.

After the exams, she needed to do an internship in a CA firm. In Kolkata, there were many good CA firms. So, she was just waiting to get into the best of the CA firms so that she could learn the traits of the practical portion.

12(iii) First Time Leaving Kolkata:

Now, Vikrant was residing in Lucknow. So, he insisted his parents and Trisha to come over and stay with him. Trisha was reluctant because they did not know of any good CA firms. But she knew one thing if Vikrant was saying then there was no question of doubt. He will always do his best. That's why Trisha called Vikrant 'God'. Though Vikrant would say I am not God but simply a human being.

As they reached Lucknow, Vikrant had always already spoken to the best CA firm and made sure Trisha got there. Trisha gradually came to know that it was the best CA firm and didn't get through so easily. Trisha would have not asked for anything else. Vikrant is a person who does good to all irrespective of who the person is. One and half a year passed by. She had to study for her final level of CA exams.

At that time, Lucknow did not have face-to-face classes tuition was on a virtual basis. Trisha discussed with Vikrant and concluded that she would take tuition in Kolkata. By the end of 2009, she started tuition for all the practical papers except Taxation.

Trisha became super busy and studied daily. Even on Sundays, she had classes. She did not feel tired or exhausted her family was always there to support her if she scumbled.

13. *Death Arrives Reality Shows:*

Trisha would go to tuitions, come back, and write in fresh whatever she had learned from the respective subjects taken. Though she was getting the best tuition, she was not able to cope with all three subjects simultaneously. But there was no choice. Each student had opted for three subjects simultaneously and some had opted for four or five subjects too. Trisha was lucky to have two tuitions near her house and one far away.

In the first attempt of her final exams, she scored miserably. She did not know what to do. After two more attempts, she got the knack for how to prepare and give exams. In May 2012, she enrolled for both groups of the final exams. This time she had prepared for the exams very well. After taking two exams of the first group, Trisha's grandmother became very ill, and we understood that she would not be able to recover now, and it was time for us to bid her goodbye. Trisha went to see her grandma and her uncle, said to Trisha's grandmother, "Maa gives her your blessings. She is in the final stage of her exams." She put her hand on Trisha's head and blessed her. This was the last time she saw her.

Trisha was in the state of mind to give her the third paper. Though, she had done all the preparations but felt that she had done nothing. She told her father, "Papaji I will not go and give my Audit paper which was the third paper?" Her father replied, "Go and give your exam, you won't get less than zero" Don't give up on it. Her father's words got registered in her mind and this was the first time she didn't evaluate what she should get. She didn't expect or felt tense in appearing for the exam.

The exams went very well. She couldn't believe that she had written this paper without any tension. She rushed home and started studying for the last paper in the first group. She was very prepared in the last paper. So, she was not that tense, but the only issue was she should give her best. She was very calm.

She now had the presence of mind as well. Unexpectedly, the paper went well. The smile on her face could only tell her exams went fabulous.

She appeared for the final group at the same time. After giving the second group, she was quite sure of not passing.

14. Self-Motivation:

After two months, results were out and to Trisha's surprise, she cleared the first group. She was very thrilled. The first person who she told about the result was her father. She scored two hundred and one marks, just one mark more than the passing mark.

She remembered her grandma and her blessings. She also took her father's blessing who had made it a point to give the exam. Only the last group was left to become a CA, a prestigious degree.

After six months, she appeared for her exams but couldn't clear. Again, after six months, she understood the traits of how to study smartly. During the day, she studies for fourteen to sixteen hours and the remaining time she sleeps, and if still time is left, she keeps it like her leisure time. Even while sleeping, in her subconscious mind, she would decide for what will she do tomorrow.

She took her exams and not for a minute thought whether she would clear or not. The question of clearing and not clearing was not in her mind. She was very sure that she would clear her exams, and that the degree would be hers. All the family members were waiting for the results. One of her friends, called Trisha and told her that the results were out. Trisha was out and told her once she reached home would see the results.

Trisha's heart was beating very fast not because of the outcome of the exam but how much she will get in each subject. As she reached home, she opened her laptop and waited for the site to be opened. As the site opened, she entered the roll number. She had cleared all the papers but the criteria of achieving 50% was not achieved. She fell as if the floor broke and she was gone beneath it. She was short by twelve marks to be cleared. This time, Trisha broke from inside. She started to think about what she got wrong. She got no answers to her questions.

15. *Change of City:*

After two months, Vikrant was transferred to Mumbai. Trisha along with her brother and parents headed towards a new place. Aman was already there. So, the happiness of staying together was immersive. The togetherness of staying together was priceless and can't be expressed.

Again, after three months, CA exams were due. Though Trisha was preparing for the exams but not wholeheartedly. She appeared for the exam not at all seriously. The enthusiasm of adding a prefix of CA was still alive but the efforts were not at all seen. The word passion had doused off. How can the fire be lit again when the water has already been doused off? To give a last chance, Trisha and her parents went to Kolkata so that she could prepare without any distractions. Aman was completely against it because he knew she had taken so many attempts and he wanted Trisha to move forward. On the other side, Vikrant positively said, "Let her try one more time" Trisha went to Kolkata with her parents. She had a dream which she had to make it a reality. She had made many attempts, but still, she doubted her ability.

Exams came and she was quite sure that she would not clear.

Trisha flunked and this time she made it a point that she would not appear in any more exams of CA. Meanwhile she shifted to Bengaluru along with her parents. Aman got a better job in Bengaluru, so he went there. After the results, she came across a job in one of the renowned MNCs. Though she knew that she would not clear the interview, she went. After two rounds, she got selected. A total of twenty-two people were selected from 110 candidates. She felt like she had a purpose, and the dreams got wings too. She made a point that she would work with a sense of confidence and responsibility.

15(i) Joining Office:

Trisha loved her work and made friends in the office. After around one and a half years she lost her interest in continuing to work. She put down her papers. She expressed her thoughts to Vikrant. He tried to convince her by trying to say what she would do after she left the job. Trisha was very firm about leaving the job. When Aman got to know of this, he became furious and said, "You will not leave the job, you need to continue." She continued her job and after a few days, she quit.

After quitting her job, she again went into a mode of just breathing rather than living. Days passed, and Trisha would only lay down on the bed and she would only sleep. Sleeping and eating were two things she did.

In between she got to know Sunny was in Kochi and working there. One of her office colleagues who knew everything about Sunny from Trisha, asked why we not go and meet him. Trisha was sure that he would not talk and what would she say at home? Though it had been years the feeling of Sunny presence was always there in her mind. She would adore the moments they spent together. Those moments were priceless and though she was in her comfort zone but in that zone too she never forgot him. All the people in the family prayed Trisha should be back in life as soon as possible.

16. Purpose and Goal:

A few months later, when Trisha was gaining back in life, a bomb exploded. A bomb that had no sound, pollution, or threat. The bomb was Sunny's marriage. She just prayed that what she heard was just not a reality. After she saw the photos on social media, she felt as if the land had drifted apart, and she had drowned it. Till now Trisha was feeling someday they would meet but no more.

All her emotions were shattered but somehow, she convinced herself by saying even though Radha and Krishna did not marry but their love for each other is worshipped to date.

A few months later, Vikrant told Trisha, "There is a marriage proposal for you." To which Trisha replied, "All these years everybody respected her viewpoint, now it was Trisha's chance to give back."

She always told her mother, "I prayed only for becoming a CA and getting married to Sunny" Both my wishes didn't materialize. I always folded my hand towards the Almighty and ask for it. These two things asked were not granted may be which was not meant for me.

Trisha always believed in hard work rather than luck. She now started to believe with hard work the same amount of luck is also required. Luck is a very important ingredient for success in life.

That day, she realized when she did not ask for anything but only his hands on her forehead, she got everything. Now why she was asking? She will get what she deserves, she doesn't have to ask God for it. She will get the best thing ever. Trisha asked or did not ask God; she got the best results wholeheartedly.

When she achieved, she used to motivate her or if she did not achieve this too motivated her, but the only difference was that her stubbornness would be added to it. This means God gave anything she deserved and not what she asked for. All the while when. Trisha did not achieve or achieve she accepted it wholeheartedly. When Trisha achieved anything, this, motivated her, and when she did not, this too motivated her, but the only difference was that her stubbornness would be added to it. The next try would make her stronger to achieve. She was always stubborn in her life. Now the best part was she used her stubbornness for the better part of life too.

Who knows what the future upheld? Some cry about the past some cry about the future but no one lives at present. That's the only dilemma. I hope like me, people too try to find purpose and set goes to achieve. The purpose of life is to do "Karma" as defined by Shree Krishna to Arjun in the battle of

Kurukshetra. The Lord explains to Arjun that the word 'Karma' is to do your duty or to do those things for which he is born or created by God.

A goal is something a human being wants to achieve and when it is achieved it reaches its destination. Then we set other goals and try to achieve them. You should never say that purpose and goal are similar. They are completely different versions of life.

17. Sunny's Presence:

Trisha's parents along with other elders looking for a groom. She met many boys, but none materialized. Once, she was coming, she came to know Sunny was leaving apart. She was moved as to what may have happened. As soon as she told her mother, she told Trisha to talk to him. But Trisha was reluctant about what would she say or whether he would talk. She told her mom, "I don't know what to do?" Moreover, I am going to Kolkata to see a groom. Though she met the boy, nothing materialized. Somewhere she thought one day they both would be together no matter what. However, she always wondered why God was playing games with her. Ankit, a common friend of Trisha and Sunny, told Trisha about Sunny but he did himself know the reason.

One year passed, and Trisha always wanted to talk to him. But she always thought he would not talk to her. She did not dare to talk. Only God knew why. But this time she was determined to talk.

Ankit insisted, "I think you should try to connect directly rather than someone in between." She told

Ankit, "If he does not talk then? Ankit said, "Then what can you do. There is only this choice for you."

18. A Ray of Hope:

Trisha gathered all her courage and messaged Sunny. After a span of around four and five hours, he responded. He typed, "How are you?" To which Trisha replied, "I am good." She felt as if she was on cloud nine. They talked like Hi, hello and so on. One day she told Sunny can we talk. On this, he said, "I don't want any personal talks. If you want, I can talk as friends. They both knew very well they were soulmates and always be. After some time, Sunny and Trisha did not talk at all. The very hope shattered, and she knew that there would be no talking in the future. His words felt as if a last drop of blood was taken away from a person who is living on that only drop of blood. Trisha felt she lost Sunny and this time perhaps forever.

Days passed. Trisha only wished a day would come and that day would be magical as if heaven had come to meet earth. But dreams are dreams until they become reality. All these years she only wished to talk to him, but God only knows what his plan for them was. Will they ever meet or talk in this lifetime? Who knows?

19. Presence in Sub-Consciously Mind:

One day Trisha for the first time went on a trip with two friends to Vaishno Devi in Katra, Jammu and Kashmir. One of her friends asked, "Have you ever loved anyone, or somebody love you?" She said one person was there I love and always be. Neha's curiosity aroused and she wanted to know more. Trisha narrated everything and Neha assured her that she would talk to him.

After the trip, she called as promised. Neha called Trisha and told her, "You should take off your mind for Sunny. He has no feelings for you." Trisha heard everything but the same as before, her feelings for Sunny remained the same just like an unmoved stone.

Trisha did not know with the passage of time; memories of Sunny became more and more craved in the mind just as a stone craved in a monument. Do we ever think about why we like or dislike a person? There must be some reason. Isn't it? All these years have passed but the longing to meet and speak to Sunny has not faded at all.

After six months, the same feeling aroused. The feeling of talking to Sunny and telling him that she was not selfish or indifferent to their relationship. But all these years, she didn't get any opportunity to express her unburied feelings. This time she called more than fifteen times on Sunny's mobile number. As usual, he did not pick up the call. Then she called a common friend, Vishal, and requested him to convince Sunny to talk once. After talking to Vishal added, " I want to tell you he will not. So, move forward and forget about him." It's been sixteen years. Don't bother with your past, live in the present, and don't brood over the future. It's been ages since you had any conversation, Why do you want to talk? I am your friend too and I want to tell you that out of the way, he would talk only as a friend." Trisha found a ray of hope. She called Sunny again and same as before he did not pick up.

She spoke to Vishal again and he told Trisha, he would not talk either as a friend or otherwise. Trisha in a depressed way answered, "But you told me he will talk if I talk as a friend." Vishal insisted, "Trisha, I can tell you bluntly, Sunny has a lot of responsibility towards his family, and he is going through a lot of problems," You don't add one more burden.

Trisha felt helpless but after so many years, the time spent with Sunny was the same as if it just happened a moment before.

19(i) Ankit's Words:

There was not a single day in Trisha's life when she didn't remember Sunny. Ankit one day said he met Sunny and Vishal. Immediately, Trisha in a curious matter, asked "What did talk about" He said "Nothing specific. But as I was about to speak, he insisted that he did not want to talk anything about Trisha?" When Ankit met Trisha he said, "It has been twenty-four years since you people met and eighteen years when you parted ways and had no conversation at all. Why don't you move on and let him live his life too? If there was even a 1% chance, I would tell you to move forward but he has no feelings for you. You are a mature person and not a college student or a teenager, forgot everything please."

Trisha at that night could not sleep and wrote a mail stating that forgive me and please forget what happened at their last meeting. I wanted to say I am not selfish or indifferent. I just want to say this.

Trisha didn't know whether he read that mail or not. He must have because Ankit called Trisha and asked did you write a mail to Sunny. To which she said 'Yes' but how did you know? Sunny furiously called me stating "Why did you give my email ID? How did you get the mail email ID?" Trisha stated "It is difficult to get one's mobile number or an email ID. Please I request." Ankit said, "Let him live and you live too."

20. Truth Is Ultimate:

Trisha does not know whether she will ever become a CA, or she will ever get married to Sunny. One thing she learned about life was past is true in the sense that it has happened, so we have facts of things. It's like in history. We talk about it as there is evidence of what happened. So, it is true. The future is about to happen so we don't know what will happen. The present is completely true because, at that very moment, things can be viewed and felt.

We all know the past is what is gone, the future is about to come, and the present is a moment you are living. It is rightly said, "Concentrate on your present you will make history in the true sense."

Have you ever heard, 'Time flies' you must have. Do you know why? It is so because time runs all the while and doesn't stop for anybody. Time is passed, time to come is yet to come and you are living now.

Stay for the present and you will live your best life. I assure you will continue and utilize life fully and build the best life for yourself. Your life will be an example for others, and they too will follow your steps and help to better their life.

In Bhagavata Gita, Shree Krishna told Arjun "Karma kar phal ki chinta mat kar"

(Do your work diligently and don't think of the results). It's also said that work is completely in your hands but don't brood over the results which is not at all in your capacity.

Purpose and Goals

Trisha spent forty years of her life understanding the facts of the past, present, and future. She is highly delighted at least she experienced this in her lifetime.

People spend all their lives finding their purpose and goal of being on this planet. Purpose refers to 'Karma' that you do continuously till you achieve salvation, and the goal is the ultimate solution you do on the path of the journey till you achieve your destination.

One after one you set a goal for yourself, and the person tries to achieve it. Not all the goals need to be achieved. Some goals are achieved, and some may not. The goals that are achieved become individual successes and those that are not achieved are called failures.

But I want to ask, things not achieved are failures? No not at all. It is a failure because that is an unfulfilled goal that can be used in another goal and will be known as an experience for the new one. Trisha understood one thing, her not becoming a CA or not meeting Sunny is common. It is true that if I had become a CA, I wouldn't be writing this book and for Sunny, you never know if they cross paths again because Love comes naturally. Let's hope for the best and live your life to the fullest. You don't know what life bestows on you. Live long and live healthy. That should be only the mantra of life. Do what is right and 'NEVER' tell a lie in any situation. Always respect your parents because they are the ones who brought you into this world. Show empathy rather than sympathy to every living being.

Life will be as beautiful as a peacock who spreads her feathers when rains shower on the earth. Life is as beautiful as a drop of water that falls on a leaf. Everything is beautiful, just try to see it from a different perspective, and you can make your life as beautiful thing as ever.

The very purpose and goals of life should ultimately source of being. I just want to add, that as I understood my life's being, I hope you too find your goals and purpose in life. Change according to time is necessary and be the change you want to see.

> "*To exist is to change*
> *To change is to mature*
> *To mature is to go on*
> *Creating oneself endlessly*
> *- Henri Bergson*
> *French Philosopher*
> *(1895- 1941)*"

> "*The secret of change is to focus all your energy, not on fighting the old but on building the new*
> *- Socrates*"

Acknowledge

I would thank all my family members including the ones who are not physical present as well. I personally thank my nephew, Pravit who believed that I could write a book. I dedicate the foundation of the book to Pranay and Pravit who helped in proof reading and Bhavya, my niece and Pravit who helped on cover page and back cover.

I thank my parents, my brothers Rakesh and Ashish for believing in me. I want to give my regards to my English teacher Mr. Melvin deDoncker and Ms.P.Bano and Miss Mala who helped me get used to reading novels.

Acknowledging every individual is not possible. They are many people who have crossed my life at every phase. At last, I would like to give my heartiest regards to all those people who I missed.